yoga
friends

a pose-by-pose partner adventure for kids

Mariam Gates & Rolf Gates

ILLUSTRATED BY

Sarah Jane Hinder

sounds true
BOULDER, COLORADO

When I am with you
and you are with me,
together we become
what we want to be.

We sit back to back and take a deep breath in.

Then let it out slowly and we're ready to begin.

We are a feathery owl gazing
down to the ground.

A twist to each side and we
see all the way around.

We are a lizard on a rock basking in the sun.

Back and forth we go until our rest is done.

OCTOPUS
octopoda

One small turn and we're an octopus
swimming silently so as not to cause alarm.

We move slowly under the water,
arm after arm after arm.

Another shift and we're face to face
and toes to toes.

Now we're a sailboat
skimming across the waves as it goes.

Next we turn into a drawbridge and balance
by looking right into each other's eyes.

Holding not too loose and not too tight,
we help each other rise.

We are stronger together.
Hand in hand,
we spread out wide.

Leaning in, we curve to form a heart
with each of us as one side.

Now we grow into a tree
with deep roots and limbs
that reach the sky.

Standing tall, we are quiet and still
as the busy world moves by.

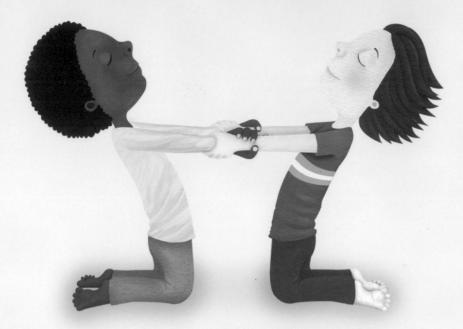

When I am with you
and you are with me,
together we become
what we want to see.

What else can we be?

the yoga friend flow

Lotus

Sit back to back with your partner and grow tall through your spine. Rest your hands on your knees or in your lap.

Lizard

Hook your arms behind you with your partner's arms, elbow to elbow. One of you slowly leans forward while the other leans back. Then switch, so you are stretching back and forth.

Octopus

One partner turns around so you are both facing the same direction. Stretch and move your arms and legs in the air.

Owl

Each of you reach back and place a hand on your partner's knee. Bring your other arm across your body and rest your hand on your own knee. Gently twist your body from side to side.

Boat

Turn to face each other and bend your knees. Bring the soles of your feet together, one at a time.

Then try lifting your feet toward the sky. You can hold hands or use your hands behind you for balance.

Drawbridge

Still facing each other, plant your feet on the ground. Bend your knees and reach out to hold your partner's hands to help each other balance and rise.

Heart

Lean in toward your partner. Straighten your bottom arm to bring your hands together low to form the tip of the heart. Reach your top hand over your head and hold or touch your partner's hand to form the top of the heart. Keep your top elbow bent and bend your outer knee.

Double Warrior

With both of you facing forward, hold your partner's hand or wrist. Bring your inside foot next to your partner's and step out to the side with your outside foot. Bend your outer knee, and reach and lean out wide.

Tree

Still standing side by side, place your hand on your partner's back. Bring your outer leg out to the side and then rest your foot on the shin or thigh of your inner leg. Bring your other hand in front of you to meet your partner's, palm to palm.

Tree Variation

Bring your inside hand to meet your partner's, palm to palm. Bring your outer leg out to the side and then rest your foot on the shin or thigh of your inner leg. Stretch your outside arm out, palm facing forward and elbow bent.

Mirror Me

Stand or sit facing your partner a couple of feet apart. One will be the leader first, and the other will be the mirror. Then you will switch. Look right into your partner's eyes. You will be communicating without talking so having eye contact will help.

The leader begins by making slow, smooth movements. The mirror follows these exactly. When you are working well together, it will appear like the two of you really are images in a mirror. The leader is in charge of moving at a pace that can be easily followed. The mirror is in charge of paying attention.

Leader, try lifting one arm high over your head. Then lift the other arm. Bring both arms straight out to the sides and hold them there for a moment. Then bring them back down.

Try nodding gently yes and then in slow motion shaking your head no. Try slowly making a funny face for your partner to copy.

Now try something new. Stand up and bend your knees or pick your foot up off the ground. See what happens when you lean to one side and then the other or even try twisting your whole body.

When you are ready, switch roles of leader and mirror. Which role is easier or harder to do? Why? Be sure to thank your partner with a slow mirror high-five.

For Max Milton Wheeler Korn
& Benjamin Wheeler Goldberg.
A perfect pair.
MG + RG

For my beautiful granddaughter Mila.
May your world be full
of yoga friends.
SJH

Sounds True, Boulder, CO 80306

Copyright © 2018 Mariam Gates and Rolf Gates
Illustrations © 2018 Sarah Jane Hinder

Published 2018

Book design by Ranée Kahler
Cover design by Karen Polaski

Printed in South Korea

Library of Congress Cataloging-in-Publication Data

Names: Gates, Mariam, author. | Gates, Rolf, author. | Hinder, Sarah Jane,
  illustrator.
Title: Yoga friends : a pose-by-pose partner adventure for kids /
  Mariam Gates and Rolf Gates ; illustrated by Sarah Jane Hinder.
Description: Boulder, CO : Sounds True, 2018. | Audience: Age 4-8.
Identifiers: LCCN 2017030912 (print) | LCCN 2017039812 (ebook) |
  ISBN 9781622038176 (ebook) | ISBN 9781622038169 (hardcover)
Subjects: LCSH: Hatha yoga for children—Juvenile literature. |
  Yoga—Juvenile literature.
Classification: LCC RJ133.7 (ebook) | LCC RJ133.7 .G43 2018 (print) |
  DDC 613.7/046083—dc23
LC record available at https://lccn.loc.gov/2017030912

10 9 8 7 6 5 4 3 2 1